Favorite Fairy Tales

TOLD IN IRELAND

Favorite Fairy Tales

TOLD IN IRELAND

DISCARDED

Retold from Irish Storytellers

by Virginia Haviland

Illustrated by Catharine O'Neill

A Beech Tree Paperback Book *New York*

First Beech Tree Edition, 1994, published by arrangement with Little, Brown and Co.
Printed in the United States of America

10 9 8 7 6 5 4 3

These stories have been adapted from the following sources:

By permission of Mrs. Seumas MacManus:

"The Bee, the Harp, the Mouse, and the Bum-Clock" and "The Old Hag's Long Leather Bag," from *Donegal Fairy Stories* by Seumas MacManus (Garden City, New York: Doubleday, Page and Company, 1900).

"Billy Beg and the Bull," from *In Chimney Corners*, by Seumas MacManus (Garden City, New York: Doubleday, Page and Company, 1899).

By permission of Ruth Sawyer Durand:

"The Widow's Lazy Daughter," as told to Ruth Sawyer "under a lazy bush in Donegal by a wandering tinker" (hitherto unpublished).

"Patrick O'Donnell and the Leprechaun," as told to Ruth Sawyer by Patrick O'Donnell's great-granddaughter Dorothy Donelly (hitherto unpulished).

Library of Congress Cataloging-in-Publication Data

Haviland, Virginia, 1911-1988
    Favorite fairy tales told in Ireland / retold from Irish storytellers by Virginia
Haviland ; illustrated by Catharine O'Neill.
        p.   cm.
    Summary: Presents five tales: The bee, the harp, the mouse, and the bum-clock; The old hag's long leather bag; Billy Beg and the bull; The widow's lazy daughter; and Patrick O'Donnell and the leprechaun.
    ISBN 0-688-12598-0 (pbk.)
    1. Fairy tales — Ireland.   2. Tales — Ireland.   [1. Fairy tales.
2. Folklore — Ireland.]   I. O'Neill, Catharine, 1950-   ill.   II. Title.
PZ8.H295Faviag 1994
[398.21' 09415]—dc20   94–84
                                      CIP
                                      AC

Minor editorial and style changes have been made in the stories for these new editions.

Contents

The Bee, the Harp, the Mouse, and the Bum-clock

O NCE A WIDOW HAD A SON named Jack. Jack and his mother owned just three cows. They lived well and were happy for a long time, but at last hard times came down on them. Their crops failed, and poverty looked in at the door. Indeed, things got so bad for the widow, she had to make up her mind to sell one of their three cows.

"Jack," she said one night, "in the morning you must go to the fair to sell the branny cow."

In the morning brave Jack was up early. He took a stick in his fist and turned out the cow, and off he went with her.

When Jack came to the fair, he saw a great crowd gathered in a ring in the street. He went into the crowd to see what they were looking at. There in the middle of them he saw a wee man with a wee, wee harp, a mouse, a cockroach, which is called a bum-clock, and a bee to play on the harp.

When the man put them down on the ground and whistled, the bee began to play the harp. The mouse and the bum-clock stood up on their hind legs and got hold of each other and began to waltz. And as soon as the harp began to play and the mouse and the bum-clock to dance, there wasn't a man or woman, or a thing in the fair, that didn't begin to dance also. The pots and pans and the wheels and reels jumped and jigged all over the town, and Jack himself and the branny cow danced as much as the next. There was never a town in such a state before or since.

After a while the man picked up the bee, the harp, the mouse, and the bum-clock and put them into his pocket. The men and women, Jack and the cow, the pots and pans, the wheels and reels that had hopped and jigged now stopped, and every one began to laugh as if to break his heart.

The man turned to Jack. "Jack," said he, "how would you like to be master of all these animals?"

"Why," said Jack, "I should like it fine."

"Well, then," said the man, "how will we make a bargain about them?"

"I have no money," said Jack.

"But you have a fine cow," said the man. "I will give you the bee and the harp for it."

"Oh, but," said Jack, "my poor mother at home is very sad entirely. I have to sell this cow and lift her heart again."

"And better than this she cannot get," said the man. "For when she sees the bee play the harp, she will laugh if she never laughed in her life before."

"Well," said Jack, "that will be grand."

He made the bargain. The man took the cow, and Jack started home with the bee and the harp in his pocket. When he came home, his mother welcomed him back.

"And Jack," said she, "I see you have sold the cow."

"I have done that," said Jack.

"Did you do well?" said the mother.

"I did well, and very well," said Jack.

"How much did you get for her?"

"Oh," said he, "it was not for money at all I sold her, but for something far better."

"Oh, Jack! Jack!" said she. "What have you done?"

"Just wait until you see, Mother," said he, "and you will soon say I have done well."

Out of his pocket he took the bee and the harp

and set them in the middle of the floor, and whistled to them. As soon as he did this the bee began to play the harp. The mother looked at them and let a big, great laugh out of her, and she and Jack began dancing and jigging. The pots and pans, the wheels and reels also began to dance and jig over the floor. And the house itself hopped about, too.

When Jack picked up the bee and the harp again, the dancing all stopped, and his mother laughed for a long time. But when she came to herself, she got very angry entirely with Jack, and she told him he was a silly, foolish fellow. There was neither food nor money in the house, and now he had lost one of her good cows, also.

"We must do something to live," said she. "Over to the fair you must go tomorrow morning and take the black cow with you and sell her."

Off at an early hour brave Jack started, and he never halted until reaching the fair.

When he came into the fair, he saw a big crowd gathered in a ring in the street. Said Jack to himself, "I wonder what they are looking at." Into the crowd he pushed, and saw the wee man this day again with a mouse and a bum-clock.

When the man put them down in the street and whistled, the mouse and the bum-clock stood up on their hind legs and got hold of each other. They began to dance there and jig. As they did, there was not a man or woman in the street who didn't begin to jig also. Jack and the black cow, the wheels and the reels, and the pots and pans — all of them were jigging and dancing all over the town. And the houses themselves were jumping and hopping about, too. Such a place Jack or anyone else never saw before.

When the man lifted the mouse and the bum-clock into his pocket, they all stopped dancing and settled down.

The man turned to Jack. "Jack," said he, "I am glad to see you. How would you like to have these animals?"

"I should like well to have them," said Jack, "only I cannot."

"Why not?" asked the man.

"Oh," said Jack, "I have no money, and my poor

mother is very downhearted. She sent me to the fair to sell this cow and bring some money to lift her heart."

"Oh," said the man, "if you want to lift your mother's heart, I will sell you the mouse. When you set the bee to play the harp and the mouse to dance to it, your mother will laugh if she never laughed in her life before."

"But I have no money," said Jack, "to buy your mouse."

"I don't mind," said the man, "I will take your cow for it."

Poor Jack was so taken with the mouse and had so set his mind on it, that he thought it was a grand bargain entirely. He gave the man his cow, and took the mouse and started off for home. When he got home his mother welcomed him.

"Jack," said she, "I see you have sold the cow."

"I did that," said Jack.

"Did you sell her well?" asked she.

"Very well indeed," said Jack.

"How much did you get for her?"

"I didn't get money," said he, "but some-thing far better."

"Oh, Jack! Jack!" said she. "What do you mean?"

"I will soon show you that, Mother," said he, taking the mouse out of his pocket along with the harp and the bee, and he set them all on the floor. When he began to whistle, the bee began to play, and the mouse got up on its hind legs and began to dance and jig. The mother gave such a hearty laugh as she never laughed in her life before. And she and Jack began dancing and jigging. The pots and pans and wheels and reels also began to dance and jig over the floor. And the house itself hopped all about, too.

When they were tired of this, Jack lifted the harp and the mouse and the bee and put them in his pocket, and his mother laughed for a long time.

But when she came to herself, she got very angry entirely with Jack.

"Oh, Jack!" she said. "You are a stupid, good-for-nothing fellow. We have neither money nor meat in the house, and here you have lost two of my good cows, and I have only one left now. Tomorrow morning," she said, "you must be up early and take this cow to the fair and sell her. See you get something this time to lift my heart up."

"I will do that," said Jack. And so he went to his bed.

★ ★ ★

Early in the morning Jack was up and turned out the spotty cow, and went again to the fair.

When Jack came into the fair, he saw a crowd gathered in a ring in the street. "I wonder what they are looking at, anyhow," said he. He pushed through the crowd, and there he saw the same wee man he had seen before, with a bum-clock.

When the man put the bum-clock on the ground, he whistled, and the bum-clock began to dance. And as soon as the bum-clock began to dance, the men, women, and children in the street and Jack and the spotty cow began to dance and jig also. Everything on the street and about it, the wheels and reels, the pots and pans, began to jig. And the houses themselves began to dance too.

When the man lifted the bum-clock and put it in his pocket, everybody stopped jigging and dancing and laughed loud. The wee man turned and saw Jack.

"Jack, my brave boy," said he, "you will never be right-fixed until you have this bum-clock, for it is a very fancy thing to have."

"Oh, but," said Jack, "I have no money."

"No matter for that," said the man, "you have a cow, and that is as good as money to me."

"Well," said Jack, "I have a poor mother who is

very downhearted at home. She sent me to the fair to sell this cow and raise some money and lift her heart."

"Oh, but Jack," said the wee man, "this bum-clock is the very thing to lift her heart. When you put down your harp and bee and mouse on the floor, and put the bum-clock along with them, she will laugh if she never laughed in her life before."

"Well, that is surely true," said Jack, "and I think I will make a swap with you."

So Jack gave the cow to the man, and took the bum-clock himself, and started for home. His mother was glad to see Jack back.

"And Jack," said she, "I see that you have sold the cow."

"I did that, Mother."

"Did you sell her well, Jack?" said his mother.

"Very well indeed, Mother," said Jack.

"How much did you get?" said his mother.

"I didn't take any money for her, Mother, but something far better," said Jack. He took out of his pocket the bum-clock and the mouse, the bee and the harp, and set them on the floor and began to whistle. The bee began to play the harp, and the mouse and the bum-clock stood up on their hind legs and began to dance, and Jack's mother laughed very hearty. Everything in the house, the wheels and the reels and the pots and pans, went jigging and hopping over the floor. And the house itself went jigging and hopping about likewise.

When Jack lifted up the animals and put them in his pocket, everything stopped, and the mother laughed for a good while. But after a bit, when she came to herself, she saw what Jack had done and how they were without money, or food, or a cow. She got very, very angry at Jack. She scolded him hard and then sat down and began to cry.

Poor Jack, when he looked at himself, confessed that he was a stupid fool entirely.

"And what," said he, "shall I now do for my poor mother?"

One day soon, Jack went out along the road, thinking and thinking, and he met a wee woman who said, "Good morrow to you, Jack. How is it you are not trying for the daughter of the King of Ireland?"

"What do you mean?" said Jack.

Said she, "Didn't you hear what the whole world has heard, that the King of Ireland has a daughter who hasn't laughed for seven years? He has promised to give her in marriage, and to give the kingdom along with her, to any man who will take three laughs out of her."

"If that is so," said Jack, "it is not here I should be."

Back to the house he went, and gathered together the bee, the harp, the mouse, and the bum-clock. Putting them into his pocket, he bade his mother good-by. He told her it wouldn't be long till she got good news from him, and off he hurried.

When Jack reached the castle, there was a ring of spikes all round and men's heads on nearly every spike there.

"What heads are these?" Jack asked one of the King's soldiers.

"Any man that comes here trying to win the King's daughter, and fails to make her laugh three times, he loses his head and has it stuck on a spike. These are the heads of the men that failed," said he.

"A mighty big crowd," said Jack. Then Jack sent word to tell the King's daughter and the King that there was a new man who had come to win her.

In a very little time the King and the King's daughter and the King's Court all came out. They sat themselves down on gold and silver chairs in front of the castle, and ordered Jack to be brought in until he should have his trial.

Jack, before he went, took out of his pocket the

bee, the harp, the mouse, and the bum-clock. He gave the harp to the bee, and he tied a string to one and the other. He took the end of the string himself, and marched into the castle yard before all the Court, with his animals coming on a string behind him.

When the Queen and the King and the Court saw poor ragged Jack with his bee, his mouse, and with his bum-clock hopping behind him on a string, they set up one roar of laughter that was long and loud enough. And when the King's daughter herself lifted her head to see what they were laughing at, and saw Jack and his menagerie, she opened her mouth and let out such a laugh as was never heard before.

Jack made a low bow, and said, "Thank you, my lady. You have given me one of the three laughs."

Then he drew up his animals in a circle and began to whistle. The minute he did so, the bee began to play the harp. The mouse and the bum-

clock stood up on their hind legs, got hold of each other, and began to dance. The King and the King's Court and Jack himself began to dance and jig, and everything about the King's castle — pots and pans, wheels and reels — and the castle itself began to dance also. And the King's daughter, when she saw this, opened her mouth again. She let out of her a laugh twice louder than before.

Jack, in the middle of his jigging, made another bow and said, "Thank you, my lady. You have given me two of the three laughs."

Jack and his animals went on playing and dancing. But Jack could not get the third laugh out of the King's daughter, and the poor lad saw his big head in danger of going on the spike.

Then the brave mouse came to Jack's help and wheeled around upon its heel. As it did so, its tail swiped into the bum-clock's mouth, and the bum-clock began to cough and cough and cough.

When the King's daughter saw this, she opened

her mouth again, and she let out the loudest and hardest and merriest laugh that was ever heard before or since.

"Thank you, my lady," said Jack, making another bow. "I have won you all."

When Jack stopped his animals, the King took him and the animals within the castle. Jack was washed and combed. He was dressed in a suit of silk and satin, with all kinds of gold and silver ornaments, and then was led before the King's daughter. And true enough, she confessed that a handsomer and finer fellow than Jack she had never seen. She was very willing to be his wife.

Jack sent for his poor old mother and brought her to the wedding, which lasted nine days and nine nights, and every night was better than the other.

The Old Hag's Long Leather Bag

O NCE UPON A TIME, long, long ago, a widow woman had three daughters. When their father died, their mother thought they would never be in want, for he had left her a long leather bag filled with gold and silver. But he was not long dead, when an old hag came begging one day and stole the long leather bag filled with gold and silver. She went out of the country with it, no one knew where.

From that day, the widow woman had a hard struggle to bring up her three daughters.

When they were grown, the eldest said one day, "Mother, I'm a young woman now, and it's a shame for me to be here doing nothing to help you or myself. Bake me a bannock and I'll go away to push my fortune."

The mother baked her a bannock, and asked would she have half of it with her blessing or the whole of it without. The girl answered that she would take the whole without the blessing.

Off she went, after saying that if she was not back in a year and a day, they would know she was doing well, and making her fortune.

She traveled away and away, farther than I could tell you, and twice as far as you could tell me, until she came into a strange country.

Going up to a little house, the girl found an old

hag living in it. When the hag asked where she was going, she said, "I'm on my way to push my fortune."

"How would you like to stay here with me?" asked the hag. "I'm needing a maid myself."

"What will I have to do?"

"You will have to wash me and dress me, and sweep the hearth clean. But on the peril of your life, don't you ever look up the chimney," answered the hag.

"All right," she agreed.

The next day, when the hag arose, the girl washed her and dressed her, and when the hag went out, she swept the hearth clean. But she thought it would do no harm to have one wee look up the chimney. And what did she see but her own mother's long leather bag of gold and silver! She took it down at once, and, getting it on her back, started away for home as fast as she could run.

She had not gone far when she met a horse grazing in a field. When he saw her, he called out,

"Rub me! Rub me! I haven't been rubbed these seven years."

But she only struck him with a stick and drove him out of her way.

She had not gone much farther when she met a sheep. "Oh, shear me! Shear me!" begged the sheep. "I haven't been shorn these seven years."

But she struck the sheep, and sent it scurrying out of her way.

She had not gone much farther when she met a goat. "Oh, change my tether! Change my tether!" cried the goat. "It hasn't been changed these seven years."

But she flung a stone at him, and went on.

Next she came to a mill. The mill cried out, "Oh, turn me! Turn me! I haven't been turned these seven years."

But she did not heed what it said. She only went in and lay down behind the mill door, with the bag under her head, for it was then night.

When the hag came into her hut again, she saw that the girl was gone. Over to the chimney she ran, to see if the girl had carried off the bag. In a great rage because it was missing, she started to run as fast as she could after her.

She had not gone far when she met the horse, and asked, "Oh, horse, horse of mine, did you see this maid of mine, with my tig, with my tag, with my long leather bag, and all the gold and silver I have earned since I was a maid?"

"Aye," said the horse, "it is not long since she passed here."

The hag ran on and on, until she met the sheep. "Sheep, sheep of mine, did you see this maid of mine, with my tig, with my tag, with my long leather bag, and all the gold and silver I have earned since I was a maid?"

"Aye," said the sheep, "it is not long since she passed here."

So she went on and on, until she met the goat.

"Goat, goat of mine, did you see this maid of mine, with my tig, with my tag, with my long leather bag, and all the gold and silver I have earned since I was a maid."

"Aye," said the goat, "it is not long since she passed here."

The hag went on farther, until she met the mill. "Mill, mill of mine, did you see this maid of mine, with my tig, with my tag, with my long leather bag, and all the gold and silver I have earned since I was a maid?"

And the mill answered, "Yes, she is sleeping behind the door."

The hag went in and struck the girl with a white rod, which turned her into a stone. She then lifted the bag of gold and silver onto her back, and went away home.

A year and a day went by after the eldest daughter left home. Since she had not returned, the second daughter now spoke up. "My sister must be doing well and making her fortune. Isn't it a shame for me to be sitting here doing nothing, either to help you, Mother, or myself? Bake me a bannock and I'll go away to push my fortune."

The mother did this, and asked her if she would have half the bannock with her blessing or the whole bannock without.

The girl answered that she would take the whole bannock without the blessing. As she went off she added, "If I am not back here in a year and a day, you may be sure that I am doing well and making my fortune."

She traveled away and away, farther than I could tell you, and twice as far as you could tell me, until she came into a strange country.

There, now, with this second daughter, all happened as it had before with the eldest. She too was struck with the hag's white rod and turned into a stone. And the hag lifted the bag of gold and silver onto her back, and went away home once more.

When the second daughter had been gone a year and a day, the youngest daughter said, "My two sisters must be doing very well indeed, and making great fortunes. It's a shame for me to be sitting here doing nothing, either to help you, Mother, or myself. Make me a bannock and I will go away and push my fortune."

The mother did this, and asked her if she would have half of the bannock with her blessing or the whole bannock without.

The girl answered, "I will have half of the bannock with your blessing, Mother."

The mother gave her a blessing and half a bannock, and off she went.

She traveled away and away, farther than I could tell you and twice as far as you could tell me, until she came to a strange country.

Going up to a little house, this daughter, too, met the old hag, and agreed to work as her maid.

All went the same with her as with her two

sisters, until she began running away with the long leather bag of gold and silver.

When she got to the horse, the horse called out, "Rub me! Rub me! For I haven't been rubbed these seven years."

"Oh, poor horse, poor horse," the kind youngest daughter said at once. "I'll surely do that." She laid down her bag, and rubbed the horse.

Then she went on, and it wasn't long before she met the sheep. "Oh, shear me, shear me!" begged the sheep. "I haven't been shorn these seven years."

"Oh, poor sheep, poor sheep," she answered. "I'll surely do that." She laid down the bag, and sheared the sheep.

On she went till she met the goat. "Oh, change my tether! Change my tether!" cried the goat. "It hasn't been changed these seven years."

"Oh, poor goat, poor goat," she said. "I'll surely do that."

She laid down the bag, and changed the goat's tether.

At last she reached the mill. "Oh, turn me! Turn me!" cried the mill. "I haven't been turned these seven years."

"Oh, poor mill, poor mill," she replied. "I'll surely do that." And she turned the mill.

As night was on her now, she went in and lay down behind the mill door to sleep.

When the hag came into her hut again, she found the girl gone. Over to the chimney she ran, to see if she had carried off the bag. In a great rage because it was missing, she started to run as fast as she could after her.

She had not gone far when she met the horse and asked, "Oh, horse, horse of mine, did you see this maid of mine, with my tig, with my tag, with my long leather bag, and all the gold and silver I have earned since I was a maid?"

The horse answered, "Do you think I have nothing to do but watch your maids for you? You may go somewhere else and look."

She went on and soon came upon the sheep. "Oh, sheep, sheep of mine, have you seen this maid of mine, with my tig, with my tag, with my long leather bag, and all the gold and silver I have earned since I was a maid?"

The sheep said, "Do you think I have nothing to do but watch your maids for you? You may go somewhere else and look."

She went on till she met the goat. "Oh, goat, goat of mine, have you seen this maid of mine, with my tig, with my tag, with my long leather bag, and all the gold and silver I have earned since I was a maid?"

The goat said, "Do you think I have nothing to do but watch your maids for you? You can go somewhere else and look."

At last she came to the mill. "Oh, mill, mill of mine, have you seen this maid of mine, with my tig, with my tag, with my long leather bag, and all the gold and silver I have earned since I was a maid?"

The mill said, "Come nearer and whisper to me."

The hag went nearer to whisper to the mill—but the mill dragged her under the wheels and ground her up.

The old hag had dropped the white rod. The mill told the girl to take it and strike two stones behind the mill door. As soon as she did this, up sprang her two sisters, ready to go home. The youngest one lifted the leather bag onto her back, and the three of them traveled away and away until they reached their own land.

Their mother, who had been crying all the time they were away, was now overjoyed to see them. And rich and happy they all lived ever after.

Billy Beg
and the Bull

ONCE UPON A TIME when pigs were swine, a King and a Queen had one son, and he was called Billy Beg. Now the Queen gave Billy a bull that he was very fond of, and the bull was just as fond of him. But after some time the Queen died. Her last request to the King had been that he would never part Billy and his bull, and the King promised that come what might, come what may, he would not.

Soon the King married again. The new Queen didn't take to Billy Beg, and no more did she like the bull, seeing Billy and the bull so friendly. No way could she get the King to part Billy and the bull, so she asked a henwife what she could do.

"And what will you give me," asked the henwife, "if I very soon part them?"

"Whatever you ask," said the Queen.

"Well and good then," said the henwife. "You are to take to your bed. You must pretend that you are bad with a complaint, and I'll do the rest of it."

The Queen took to her bed and none of the doctors could do anything for her. So the Queen asked for the henwife. When the henwife came and examined the Queen, she said there was one thing, and only one, that could cure her.

The King asked what it was. The henwife said it was three mouthfuls of the blood of Billy Beg's bull. But the King wouldn't hear of this.

The next day the Queen was worse. The third

day she was worse still. She told the King she was dying, and he'd have her death on his head. So, at last, the King had to consent to the killing of Billy Beg's bull.

When Billy heard this he got very down in the heart entirely. The bull saw him looking so mournful, and asked what was wrong with him. So Billy told the bull what was wrong. The bull told him never to mind, but to keep up his heart. The Queen would never taste a drop of his blood.

The next day, when the bull was led up to be killed, he said to Billy, "Jump up on my back till we see what kind of a horseman you are."

Up Billy jumped on his back. With that the bull leaped nine miles high, nine miles deep, and nine miles broad, and came down with Billy sticking between his horns.

Hundreds were looking on dazed at the sight, and through them the bull rushed, right over the Queen, killing her dead.

Away the bull galloped, over high hills and low, over the Cove of Cork and old Tom Fox with his bugle horn.

At last they stopped. "Now then," said the bull to Billy, "put your hand in my left ear, and you'll find a napkin. When you spread it out, it will be covered with food and drink of all sorts, fit for the King himself."

Billy did this, and then he ate and drank to his heart's content. Afterwards, he rolled the napkin and put it back in the bull's ear.

"And now," said the bull, "put your hand into my right ear and you'll find a bit of a stick. If you wind it over your head three times, it will turn into a sword and give you the strength of a thousand men besides your own. When you have no more need of it as a sword, it will change back into a stick again."

Billy did all this. "Well and good," said the bull. "At twelve o'clock tomorrow I'll have to meet and fight a great bull."

Billy got up again on the bull's back. The bull started off and away, over high hills and low, over the Cove of Cork and old Tom Fox with his bugle horn.

There they stopped and Billy's bull met the other bull. Both of them fought, and the like of their fight was never seen before or since. They knocked the soft ground into hard, and the hard into soft, the soft into spring wells, the spring wells into rocks, and the rocks into high hills. They fought long, and Billy Beg's bull killed the other, and drank his blood.

Billy took the napkin out of the bull's ear again. He spread it out and ate a hearty dinner.

Then said the bull to Billy, "At twelve o'clock tomorrow, I'm to meet the brother of the bull I killed today, and we'll have a hard fight."

Billy got on the bull's back again, and the bull started off, over high hills and low, over the Cove of Cork and old Tom Fox with his bugle horn.

Here he met the bull's brother, and they set to and fought long and hard. At last Billy's bull killed the other and drank his blood.

Again, Billy took the napkin out of the bull's ear and spread it out and ate a hearty dinner.

Now said the bull to Billy, "Tomorrow at twelve o'clock I'm to fight the brother of the two bulls I killed. He's a mighty bull entirely, the strongest of them all. He's called the Black Bull of the Forest, and he'll be too much for me.

"When I'm dead," said the bull, "you, Billy, will take with you the napkin, and you'll never be hungry; and the stick, and you'll be able to overcome everything that gets in your way. And take out your knife and cut a strip off my hide, and make a belt of it. As long as you wear this belt, you cannot be killed."

Billy was very sorry to hear this. But he got up on the bull's back again, and they started off.

★ ★ ★

Sure enough, at twelve o'clock the next day they met the great Black Bull of the Forest. Both of the bulls began to fight, and they fought hard and long. But at last the Black Bull of the Forest killed Billy Beg's bull, and drank his blood.

Billy Beg was so sad at this that for two days he

sat over the bull. He neither ate nor drank, but cried salt tears all the time.

After the two days, Billy got up. He spread out the napkin and ate a hearty dinner, for he was very hungry now. Then he cut a strip off the hide of the bull and made a belt for himself. Taking it and the bit of stick and the napkin, he set out to push his fortune.

Well now, Billy traveled for three days and three nights until at last he came to a great gentleman's place. He asked the gentleman if he could give him work, and the man said he wanted just such a boy as him for herding cattle.

Billy asked what cattle would he have to herd, and what wages would he get.

The gentleman said he had three goats, three cows, three horses, and three donkeys that he fed in an orchard. Also, he said that no boy who went with them ever came back alive, for there were three giants—and these were brothers—that came to milk the cows and the goats every day. Always they killed the boy that was herding. If Billy wished to try, he could, but they wouldn't fix his wages until they'd see if he would come back alive.

"Agreed, then," said Billy.

The next morning Billy got up and drove the animals to the orchard and began to feed them. About the middle of the day he heard three terrible roars that shook the apples off the trees, shook the horns on the cows, and made the hair stand up on Billy's head.

In came a frightful big giant with three heads, who began to threaten Billy. "You're too big for one bite, and too small for two," bellowed the giant. "What will I do with you?"

"I'll fight you," answered Billy, stepping out to him and swinging the bit of stick three times over his head. The stick changed into a sword and gave him the strength of a thousand men besides his own.

But the giant laughed at the size of him. "Well, how will I kill you?" asked he. "Will it be by a swing by the back or a cut of the sword?"

"With a swing by the back," said Billy, "if you can."

They both laid hold for a wrestle, and Billy lifted the giant clean off the ground.

"Oh, have mercy," said the giant. But Billy took up his sword and killed the giant then and there.

It was evening by this time, so Billy drove home the three goats, three cows, three horses, and three donkeys. That night all the dishes in the house could not hold the milk the cows had to give.

"Well," said the gentleman, "this beats me. I never saw anyone coming back alive out of there before, nor the cows with a drop of milk. Did you see anything in the orchard?" asked he.

"Nothing worse than myself," said Billy. "And what about my wages now?"

"Well," said the gentleman, "you'll hardly come

alive out of the orchard tomorrow. So we'll wait until after that."

Next morning his master told Billy that something must have happened to one of the giants. He used to hear the cries of three giants every night, but last night he only heard two crying.

That morning, after Billy had eaten breakfast, he drove the animals into the orchard again, and began to feed them.

About twelve o'clock he heard three terrible roars that shook the apples off the trees, the horns on the cows, and made the hair stand up on Billy's head. In came a frightful big giant, with six heads. He told Billy he would make him pay for killing his brother yesterday. "You're too big for one bite, and too small for two. What will I do with you?" bellowed the giant.

Well, the long and the short of it is that Billy lifted this giant clean off the ground, too, and took up his sword and killed him then and there.

It was evening by this time, so Billy drove the animals home again. The milk the cows gave that night overflowed all the dishes in the house, and, running out, turned a rusty mill that hadn't been turned for thirty years.

If the master was surprised to see Billy come back the night before, he was ten times more surprised now. "Did you see anything in the orchard today?"

"Nothing worse than myself," said Billy. "And what about my wages now?"

"Well, never mind about your wages till tomorrow," said the gentleman. "I think you'll hardly come back alive again."

Billy went to his bed, and the gentleman went to his.

When the gentleman rose in the morning, he said to Billy, "I don't know what's wrong with two of the giants. Only one did I hear crying last night."

★ ★ ★

Well, when Billy had eaten his breakfast, he set out to the orchard once more, driving before him the animals.

Sure enough, about the middle of the day he heard three terrible roars again. In came another giant, this one with twelve heads on him.

"You villain, you," thundered the giant. "You killed my two brothers, and I'll have my revenge on you now. But you're too big for one bite, and too small for two. What will I do with you?"

Again it ended with brave Billy lifting the giant clean off the ground, and taking his sword, and killing him.

That evening Billy drove his animals home. This time the milk of the cows had to be turned into a valley, where it made a lake three miles long, and three miles broad, and three miles deep.

Now the gentleman wondered more than ever to

find Billy back alive. "Did you see nothing in the orchard today, Billy?" he asked.

"No, nothing worse than myself," said Billy.

"Well, that beats me," said the gentleman.

"What about my wages now?" asked Billy.

"Well, you're a good mindful boy," said the gentleman, "and I'll give you any wages you ask for the future."

The next morning the gentleman said to Billy, "Not one giant did I hear crying last night. I don't know what has happened to them."

★ ★ ★

That day the gentleman said to Billy, "Now you must look after the cattle again, Billy, while I go to see the fight."

"What fight?" asked Billy.

"Why," said the gentleman, "the King's daughter is going to be eaten by a fiery dragon, if the greatest fighter in the land doesn't kill the dragon first. And if he's able to kill the dragon, the King is to give him his daughter in marriage."

"That will be fine," said Billy.

Billy drove the animals to the orchard again. He had never seen the like of all the people that passed by that day to see the fight. They went in coaches and carriages, on horses and donkeys, riding and walking, crawling and creeping. One man that was passing said to Billy, "Why don't you come to see the great fight?"

"What would take the likes of me there?" said Billy.

But when Billy found them all gone, he saddled and bridled the best black horse his master had. He put on the best suit of clothes he could find in his master's house, and rode off to the fight after the rest.

When he arrived, he saw the King's daughter with the whole court about her on a platform before the castle. He had never seen anyone half so beautiful.

The great warrior that was to fight the dragon was walking up and down on the lawn before her, with three men carrying his sword. And everyone in the whole country was gathered there looking at him.

But when the fiery dragon came up with twelve heads on him and every mouth spitting fire, he let twelve roars out, and the warrior ran away and hid himself up to the neck in a well of water. No one could get him to come and face the dragon.

The King's daughter asked then if there was no one to save her from the dragon. But no one stirred.

When Billy saw this, he tied the belt of the bull's hide around him, swung his stick over his head, and went in.

After a terrible fight entirely, he killed the dragon. And then everyone gathered about to find out who the stranger was. But Billy jumped on his horse and darted away sooner than let them know. But just as he was getting away, the King's daughter pulled the shoe off his foot.

Now when the dragon was killed, the warrior that had hid in the well came out. He brought the dragon's heads to the King, and said that it was he in disguise who had killed the dragon.

But the King's daughter tried the shoe on him and found it didn't fit. And she said she would marry no one but the man the shoe fit.

When Billy got home he quickly took off the fine suit, and he had the horse in the stable and the cattle all home before his master returned.

When the master came, he began telling Billy about the wonderful day they had had entirely. He told about the grand stranger that came riding down out of a cloud on a black horse, and killed the fiery dragon, and then vanished in a cloud again.

"Now, Billy," said he, "wasn't that wonderful?"

"It was, indeed," said Billy, "very wonderful entirely."

After that it was announced over the country that all the people were to come to the King's castle on a certain day, so that the King's daughter could try the shoe on them. The one it fit, she was to marry.

★ ★ ★

When the day arrived, Billy was in the orchard with the three goats, three cows, three horses, and three donkeys, as usual.

He had never seen the like of all the crowds that passed that day going to the King's castle to try on the shoe. They all asked Billy if he was not going to the King's castle, but Billy said, "Now, what would be bringing the likes of me there?"

At last when all the others had gone, there

passed an old man wearing a scarecrow suit of rags. Billy stopped him and asked what he would take to swap clothes with him.

"Now don't be playing off your jokes on my clothes," said the old man, "or maybe I'll be making you feel my stick."

But Billy soon let him see he was in earnest, and both of them swapped suits. Billy, however, did not give up his belt.

Off to the castle started Billy, with the suit of rags on his back and an old stick in his hand. When he got there, he found everyone in great commotion trying on the shoe. Some of them were cutting down a foot, trying to get it to fit. But it was all of no use; the shoe would fit none.

The King's daughter was about to give up in despair when a ragged-looking boy, who was Billy, elbowed his way through the crowd and asked, "Let me try it on; maybe it would fit me."

But the people all began to laugh at the sight of

him. "Go along," they said, shoving and pushing him back.

But the King's daughter saw him, and called out to let him come and try on the shoe.

So Billy went up, and all the people looked on, breaking their hearts with laughing. But what would you know — the shoe fit Billy as nice as if it was made on his foot! And so the King's daughter claimed Billy as her husband. He confessed it was he who had killed the fiery dragon.

When the King had Billy dressed up in a silk and satin suit, with plenty of gold and silver on it, everyone gave in that his like they had never seen before.

Billy was married to the King's daughter, and the wedding lasted nine days, nine hours, nine minutes, nine half minutes, and nine quarter minutes; and they lived happy and well from that day to this.

The Widow's Lazy Daughter

LONG AGO there lived in Donegal a poor widow. She had one daughter, the prettiest and the laziest girl in the whole of Ireland. Not a stroke of work would she put her hand to — not from cockcrow to candletime. The poor widow worked the lee-long day to keep the cabin tidy and gather in enough food to feed the two of them.

At last the widow lost heart entirely. Leaving early one morning to do a half-day's work for a neighbor, she said to the girl, "Today you'll be doing your share of the work. You'll clean the cabin proper and make the stirabout. You'll be taking care not to burn it, for it's the last meal we have in the chest. If you burn it, the two of us will go hungry the day."

With that she was off. The girl, Eileen, watching her go, sent a great sighing after her. "Work!" said she, and she sniffed. "'Tis little liking I have for it. The longer I can put off the cleaning of the cabin the better. I'll make first the stirabout."

She built up the turf on the fire and filled up the pot with water. She hung it over the turf and stirred in the meal. Then she fetched the creepy-stool close to the hearth and sat down. With a lazy hand she began to stir, lest the meal stick to the pot and burn there. She stirred once, she stirred twice, she stirred three times. Then her hand fell to her lap and she began her dreaming.

It was always the same dream—a life with no work to it, a castle to live in, and who but the King of Ireland's son to make her his bride!

I cannot be telling you how long she dreamed; but I can tell you what fetched her out of the dreaming—a burst of smoke from the pot where the stirabout had burned to fine blackness. With the smoke came a fearsome smell. Eileen was off the stool to the door to fling it wide. And who did she find on the step, outside, waiting to be let in, but the poor widow herself. The widow saw the smoke and smelled the smell. For the first time in her life, she raised her hand against the girl. "Lass, lass, the time has come to be beating the laziness out of you." And with that she took up a stick of blackthorn and clouted the girl, out the door, down the road to the crossroads.

And who should be riding by but the King of Ireland's son, himself! He was a handsome lad and his clothes were the finest. He rode a great white horse with a red-and-gold saddlecloth and wee small golden bells on the bridle to ring his coming. He stopped, looking first at the girl and then at the widow. "'Tis a shameful thing," he said, "for a woman to be beating her own daughter. I am asking you now the why of it?"

All three waited for the widow's answer, and when it came the words tumbled from her. "'Tis sad entirely I am, to be beating the lass. But she has me troubled by all the work she does. I beat her from the spinning and she takes to the weaving; I beat her from the weaving and she takes to the knitting; I beat ...."

Here the King of Ireland's son spoke: "'Tis enough said. For a year and a day I have been riding the length and width of Ireland, searching for the prettiest lass who can work the best in the land. For my mother, the Queen, will never be letting me marry a lazy girl. So if it's all the same to you, my good woman, I'll be taking the lass to the castle, and marrying her on the morrow."

He lifted Eileen to the saddle in front of him. Then he reached in his pocket and brought out a small bag of gold. Throwing it to the widow, he said, "'Twill pay somewhat for the loss of your daughter." With that he put spurs to the white horse and the two of them were off, the wind at their back and luck following after.

When they reached the castle, the Queen met them at the door. "Here is a lass after your own heart, Mother. She is the hardest worker in all of Ireland, and the prettiest as well. What better wife can the King of Ireland's son have? Tell me that!"

The Queen looked hard and long at Eileen—at her rags, at her bare feet, and at the wildness of her hair. "She is pretty, that I grant you. But she has not the look of a lass that can work. What can she do?"

"She can spin, weave, knit—"

"Whose word did you take for it?"

"Whose but her mother's!"

The Queen shook a sorry head. "Lad, lad, you've been foolish entirely. What mother in the whole world would say but the best of her daughter?"

"But I caught her at the crossroads, beating the lass. And for why? Because she would never give over her working."

"Maybe she was beating her because she would never begin. You may well have fetched me the laziest girl in all of Ireland. Set her down from the saddle and we'll let her sleep the night. On the morrow we will give her a fair test of the work."

That night Eileen slept in a gold bed with sheets of satin under and over her. With the first of the sun the Queen woke her. "Come! You'll have your fill of tea, stirabout, and griddle bread. Then you'll be put to the spinning."

Her hunger gone, Eileen was led down a long, long corridor to a small room. Inside stood a spinning wheel and stool. Along the walls were piled stacks of flax, carded and ready. "You'll spin that flax into fine linen thread this day." With that the Queen was gone, and the door locked after her.

Eileen sat down on the stool. For the first time in her life, the shame of her laziness took her.

Deep she buried her face in her hands. Good for nothing she was. It mattered little now that the lad she loved was the King's son, that he lived in a castle, with plenty and to spare. She would lose him this day—that was all that mattered. Heavy, heavy hung the burden of that loss on her heart, and she wept—as she had never wept before.

A gentle tapping came at the window. Eileen rubbed the tears from her eyes, the better to see. There on the other side of the window stood a small woman in green with a wee red bonnet on

her head. She was tapping for the girl to let her in. Eileen sprang to her feet and opened the window. Down from the sill jumped the wee woman. "For why are you weeping, Eileen?" she asked.

"All my life I have been the laziest girl in all of Ireland. All my life I have let my poor mother work for me. Now because I cannot spin, or weave, or knit—I'll not be able to marry the King's son."

"And you love him?" asked the wee woman.

"I love him—were he nothing but a tinker on the road, without a house to hold him or a rag to cover him."

"If you will make me a promise, and keep it, I'll spin the flax for you this day."

"I will make a promise and keep it," cried the girl.

"'Tis a bargain," said the wee woman. And she took from under the cape that she wore a wee spinning wheel with a stool to match it. She told Eileen to fetch over bundles of the flax. Putting a foot on the treadle, she took an end of the flax and fastened it to the spindle. The wheel started its humming and above the humming the wee woman set a tune to the whirling of the wheel— and what she sang was this:

Turn wheel, turn about,
Spin flax, spin.
Reel, reel, faster reel,
Out and in.
Laugh, laugh, Fairies laugh,
When this is done—
I wish me at the wedding
Of the King's own son.

When the song ended, all the flax was spun and hundreds of bobbins of fine linen thread lay stacked in the room's corner.

"Don't you be forgetting, Eileen," said the wee woman, and like a wisp of green smoke she was out the window and gone.

At day's end the Queen came. She counted the bobbins in the corner. Her fingers felt the fineness and smoothness of the thread. She gave the girl a bit of smile as she said, "I see you can spin. We'll be seeing if you can weave, on the morrow."

That night the girl sat at the royal table and ate her fill. Only once did she lift her eyes to the King's son, letting the fullness of her love shine in them. "'Tis a loving lass as well as a pretty one," thought he. "What matters if she can spin and weave!"

On the morrow when the Queen took the girl to the small room, there stood a loom and a bench for the weaver, with a shuttle resting on it. "You'll wind the shuttle and begin," said the Queen. "If every bobbin is not empty at the end of the day, and the room holding lengths of fine linen cloth, you'll not be marrying my son." With that she was gone, the door locked after her.

The girl sat, thinking again of the shame of

her laziness, her head buried in her two hands. What roused her was the sound of tapping at the window. When she looked, there stood another wee woman all in green and a red bonnet on her wee head. She was beckoning to the girl to let her in. Eileen sprang to her feet and opened the window. In a thrice the wee woman was down to the floor, asking, "For why are you weeping, Eileen?"

The same answer came to the girl's tongue: "All my life I have been the laziest girl in Ireland. All my life I have let my poor mother work for me. And now—because I cannot weave, or knit—I'll never marry the King's son."

"And do you love him, Eileen?"

"I love him till my heart is near broken, thinking of the long years ahead without him."

"If you will make me a promise, and keep it, I'll be weaving the fine linen for you this day."

"I will make you any promise and keep it," said the girl.

"'Tis a bargain," said the wee woman, and she took out from under the cape that covered her a wee loom and a bench to match. From a pocket she took out a wee silver shuttle. "Fetch me the bobbins from the room's corner," she said. Then she wound the shuttle and tied the first thread. She sat herself on the bench and put her feet to the treadles. She threw her shuttle and set her song to the click of the treadles. This is what she sang:

Fly shuttle, faster fly,
Weave firm and strong,
Roll linen on the bolt
While I lilt my song.
Laugh, laugh, Fairies laugh,
When this is done,
I wish me at the wedding
Of the King's own son.

With the end of the song, every bobbin was empty. Between them Eileen and the wee woman folded the lengths of fine linen and laid them tidily upon the floor. In the flicker of a lash, the wee woman was on the sill and out the window. But as she went she said to the girl, "Don't you be forgetting, Eileen."

Then came the turn of the key in the lock, the opening of the door, and there stood the Queen. It took her no time at all to see the empty bobbins and the linen woven and folded. She felt the weave and marked the smooth-finished edge of each fold. Then she gave the girl more than half of a smile. "You can spin; you can weave. Can you knit now? We'll be trying you at it, come the morrow."

On the morrow the Queen took the girl to the small room. This time it was stacked high with skeins of yarn. She gave Eileen a pair of golden knitting needles. "You'll have all the yarn knit by day's end, or back to your mother you go." And with that the Queen was gone and the door locked behind her.

Long sat the widow's lazy daughter, making a sobbing-place of her heart. It had taken her mother more than half a week to knit a pair of stockings — and she at it the lee-long day. The girl knew it would take a mortal lass more than a year and a day to knit into stockings the stack of yarn filling the room. She buried her face deep in her hands and wept as she had never wept before.

Again the sound of tapping roused her. A third wee, wee fairy-woman in a green cape and red bonnet beckoned her to let her in.

It happened with the third as it had happened with the others. She asked, "For why are you weeping, Eileen?"

And for the third time the girl made answer. "All my life I have been the laziest girl in Ireland, letting my poor mother do all the work. And now—because I cannot knit—I'll not be able to marry the King's son."

"If you will make me a promise, and keep it, I will knit the yarn for you."

"I will make any promise and keep it!" cried the girl.

"'Tis a bargain entirely," said the wee woman. She took a creepy-stool from under her cape, and from her pocket she took a wee pair of silver knitting needles. Down she sat; and drawing to her a pile of the green skeins, she twisted a free end of yarn around her wee finger.

The next moment the needles were filling the small room with their clicking. So fast moved the wee woman's fingers that they made a blur before the girl's eyes like the quivering wings of a honey-bird. And as she knit she sang:

> *Knit, knit, needles click*
> *Work fast today,*

Stockings all on line must be

Before I'm away.

Laugh, laugh, Fairies laugh,

When this is done

I wish me at the wedding

Of the King's own son.

With the end of the song, there were more than a hundred pairs of stockings on the line. Wonderment held the girl, and never a word could she speak.

The wee woman was out the window in a thrice saying to the girl, "Don't you be forgetting, Eileen."

With the end of the day came the Queen. She looked at the stockings. She counted the pairs. For the first time since the girl had entered the castle gate, the Queen smiled the whole of her heart at her.

"In faith, you must be the best worker in all of Ireland, for you have done what no mortal hands could do. Come! On the morrow we make ready for the feast and the wedding."

The great and the grand of Ireland were asked to the wedding. Eileen wore a dress of white gossamer that had the look of moonbeams spun around her. Her veil was the finest of Irish lace; and she wore a wee golden crown on her head. After the bishop's blessing, she sat down at the royal table—between the King and the King's son.

The great feasting hall was filled, saving three empty chairs close to the royal table.

"Let the feasting begin!" cried the King. But at that very moment there came a knocking, low down, on the great door. A serving man opened it—and who should come in but a wee small woman in a green cape and a red bonnet. Every eye saw as she came down the hall that one of the wee woman's feet was enormous—ten times the size it should have been.

The King rose. "Who bid you to the wedding?"

The wee woman looked at Eileen, "I am a guest—bidden by the bride."

"Is that the truth?" asked the King.

The girl nodded. "'Tis the binding truth."

The King waved his hand to one of the empty seats. "Sit you down and welcome, wee woman that you are. But however did you come by that one monstrous foot?"

The wee woman laughed—and it made the sound of joyful bells to Eileen. "I have been spinning for hundreds of years. 'Tis the long pressing of the foot to the treadle that has made it grow."

The King's son spoke. "If that is what comes from spinning, I will never let my bride spin again."

There came another knocking at the door. When the servant man opened it, in stepped another wee woman in a green cape and a red bonnet. She came down the hall, straight for the second empty seat. As she came, everyone saw the long length of both her arms. So long were they that her fingers touched the ground as she walked.

The King spoke: "Who bid you come to the wedding?"

"Who but the bride?"

"Is that the truth?" asked the King.

"Aye, 'tis the binding truth," said the girl.

"Sit you down," said the King. "But first, tell me how you came by those monstrous long arms of yours."

"For hundreds of years I have been weaving," said the wee woman. "'Tis the throwing of the shuttle back and forth—back and forth—that has made them grow longer."

"*Aii!*" said the King's son. "If that is what comes of it, I'll never let my bride weave again."

For the third time came the knocking. All who

watched saw that the third woman had a monstrous great nose."

"Tell me," said the King, "how you came by that nose."

"For hundreds of years I have been knitting. And always I have been holding the needles closer and closer—till they've hit the nose hour after hour, and it has grown longer and fatter and redder as it is now."

"*Aii!*" said the King's son. "If that is what comes of knitting, I will never let my bride knit again." He laughed as full and hearty as the wee woman, and placed a kiss on the tip of Eileen's nose. "By this and by that, I am thinking it's not a working bride we need at all in the castle, but a pretty one. And that we have!"

The Queen looked hard at the two of them, and said too softly for aught but the King to hear, "And I am thinking that a bride who has the blessing of the fairy people is better than one who can spin, or weave, or knit."

Patrick O'Donnell
and the Leprechaun

PATRICK O'DONNELL was coming home
one night from the county fair in Donegal.
He was taking the rise in the road when he
heard off in the bogland a shrill wee cry.

Said he to himself, "'Tis not the cry of a wee
one and 'tis not the cry of a creature caught in
the furze. I will go and have a look."

So over the bog he stepped, passing one black thornbush after another, for the bog was full of them. And he came at last to the thornbush that was holding the cry.

Now there was a moon in the sky and the skies were bright, so he could see what was there. He could see to his wonderment a wee fairy man hung by the seat of his breeches on a long black thorn. He stepped closer now and asked, "How did you get yourself in this plight, wee small man that you are?"

With that he knocked his foot on something small on the ground and looked below. There he saw a wee cobbler's bench with pegs and bits of leather and with all the things of a cobbler's trade.

"Aha," he said aloud to himself and the wee man. "'Tis a leprechaun you are, wee man."

The leprechaun had stopped his squealing, and now he spoke with great impatience. "It's a small matter if I am. Take me off the blackthorn, where I'm likely to die if you don't. And take great care that you do not tear my breeches, for they are a new pair."

You can well believe that Patrick O'Donnell was filled with more than wonderment now, for he knew that the leprechaun was safe in his hands. He could ask where the crock of fairy gold was hidden, and the leprechaun by all the laws of fairy trade was bound to tell him.

So, with great care, he took the wee man by the scruff of his neck and the seat of his breeches and gently lifted him free of the blackthorn.

"Put me fast to the earth," said the wee man.

"I will not," said Patrick. "'Tis a leprechaun you are and 'tis on you I'll keep my hands and my eyes until you'll be after telling me where the pot of gold is hid."

"Have a heart," said the wee man. "What is a pot of gold to you?"

"'Tis the making of my family fortune," said Patrick O'Donnell, "and without it I am thinking we'll never have one."

There followed a long time with nought but blathering between them. In the end, with his hands still fast on the seat of his breeches and the scruff of his neck, Patrick O'Donnell went across the bog as the leprechaun directed, until they came to a certain blackthorn bush.

"'Tis here it is hid," said the leprechaun, sounding sad.

"Are you sure?" asked Patrick O'Donnell.

"I'm as sure of it as that I am the wee man who mends all the fairies' shoes after their dancing. Dig under that blackthorn yonder, and you'll find the fairies' gold."

Patrick O'Donnell looked about him under the starlight at all the blackthorn bushes on the bog and he shook his head with great hopelessness.

"I have no spade at all to dig with," said he, "and if I go home for it, how will I find which bush it is when I come back?"

"That's a trouble that's all your own," said the wee fairy man. With that a great silence fell between them.

It was Patrick himself that broke it.

"I have the answer," said he, sending up a great shout. "I'll tie my bright kerchief to the bush, and even by the starlight, dark as it is, I'll be able to tell which bush holds the crock of gold."

The fairy man set up a great chuckling. "Tie your kerchief fast now, and leave us both be going our ways."

Patrick, now sure of his family's fortune, let the leprechaun go. *Whisht!* Like a shooting star in the night, he vanished, while Patrick untied the kerchief from about his neck and tied it fast to the blackthorn bush.

It took him the rest of the night to reach home,

find himself a stout spade, and then tramp down to the bog again.

The bright orange of the sunrise was making a ring for the new day around the sky when he started across the bog. It made bright every patch of grass and stubble, furze and bush, as he tramped.

He was half across the bog when he looked about. To his great bewilderment he saw that every thornbush around him had a bright kerchief tied to it, the same as he had tied to the thornbush the leprechaun had shown him.

"If I should live to be a hundred," said Patrick O'Donnell, "I could never dig up the whole of them." So there was the ending of the O'Donnell fortune.

About This Series

I N RECENT DECADES, folk tales and fairy tales from all corners of the earth have been made available in a variety of handsome collections and in lavishly illustrated picture books. But in the 1950s, such a rich selection was not yet available. The classic fairy and folk tales were most often found in cumbersome books with small print and few illustrations. Helen Jones, then children's book editor at Little, Brown and Company, accepted a proposal from a Boston librarian for an ambitious series with a simple goal — to put an international selection of stories into the hands of children. The tales would be published in slim volumes, with wide margins and ample leading, and illustrated by a cast of contemporary artists. The result was a unique series of books intended for children to read by themselves — the Favorite Fairy Tales series. Available only in hardcover for many years, the books have now been reissued in paperbacks that feature new illustrations and covers.

The series embraces the stories of sixteen different countries: Czechoslovakia, Denmark, England, India,

France, Italy, Ireland, Germany, Greece, Japan, Scotland, Norway, Poland, Sweden, Spain, and Russia. Some of these stories may seem violent or fantastical to our modern sensibilities, yet they often reflect the deepest yearnings and imaginings of the human mind and heart.

Virginia Haviland traveled abroad frequently and was able to draw upon librarians, storytellers, and writers in countries as far away as Japan to help make her selections. But she was also an avid researcher with a keen interest in rare books, and most of the stories she included in the series were found through a diligent search of old collections. Ms. Haviland was associated with the Boston Public Library for nearly thirty years — as a children's and branch librarian, and eventually as Readers Advisor to Children. She reviewed for *The Horn Book Magazine* for almost thirty years and in 1963 was named Head of the Children's Book Section of the Library of Congress. Ms. Haviland remained with the Library of Congress for nearly twenty years, and wrote and lectured about children's literature throughout her career. She died in 1988.